HERGÉ
★
THE ADVENTURES OF
TINTIN
★

THE CALCULUS AFFAIR

EGMONT

The TINTIN books are published in the following languages:

Alsacien	CASTERMAN
Basque	ELKAR
Bengali	ANANDA
Bernese	EMMENTALER DRUCK
Breton	AN HERE
Catalan	CASTERMAN
Chinese	CASTERMAN/CHINA CHILDREN PUBLISHING
Corsican	CASTERMAN
Danish	CARLSEN
Dutch	CASTERMAN
English	EGMONT UK LTD/LITTLE, BROWN & CO.
Esperanto	ESPERANTIX/CASTERMAN
Finnish	OTAVA
French	CASTERMAN
Gallo	RUE DES SCRIBES
Gaumais	CASTERMAN
German	CARLSEN
Greek	CASTERMAN
Hebrew	MIZRAHI
Indonesian	INDIRA
Italian	CASTERMAN
Japanese	FUKUINKAN
Korean	CASTERMAN/SOL
Latin	ELI/CASTERMAN
Luxembourgeois	IMPRIMERIE SAINT-PAUL
Norwegian	EGMONT
Picard	CASTERMAN
Polish	CASTERMAN/MOTOPOL
Portuguese	CASTERMAN
Provençal	CASTERMAN
Romanche	LIGIA ROMONTSCHA
Russian	CASTERMAN
Serbo-Croatian	DECJE NOVINE
Spanish	CASTERMAN
Swedish	CARLSEN
Thai	CASTERMAN
Tibetan	CASTERMAN
Turkish	YAPI KREDI YAYINLARI

TRANSLATED BY
LESLIE LONSDALE-COOPER AND MICHAEL TURNER

EGMONT
We bring stories to life

Artwork copyright © 1956 by Editions Casterman, Paris and Tournai.
Copyright © renewed 1984 by Casterman.
Text copyright © 1960 by Egmont UK Limited.
First published in Great Britain in 1960 by Methuen Children's Books.
This edition published in 2002 by Egmont UK Limited,
239 Kensington High Street, London W8 6SA.

Library of Congress Catalogue Card Numbers Afor 21343 and R 256-462

ISBN 978 1 4052 0629 7
ISBN 1 4052 0629 2

Printed in Spain
5 7 9 10 8 6

THE CALCULUS AFFAIR

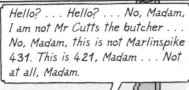

Hello? . . . Hello? . . . No, Madam, I am not Mr Cutts the butcher . . . No, Madam, this is not Marlinspike 431. This is 421, Madam . . . Not at all, Madam.

It's preposterous!

That's about the tenth time . . .

RRRING

Again?

Hello? . . . No, Madam, I am not Mr Cuts the butcher! . . . I beg your pardon? . . .

Oh! Excuse me, I . . . er . . . Captain Haddock? I'm afraid he's not in. He's gone for a walk.

. . . And from now on, all I want is my daily stroll . . . No more travels or adventures; no more careering all round the world . . . I've had enough of it!

That's what you say, Captain, but . . .

No, no, this time I'm quite serious. All I want now is to settle down in peace and quiet . . .

Ah, peace and quiet! . . . How quiet it is here . . . just listen to it . . .

BRROM

? ?

So much for your peace and quiet, Captain! Look over there. There's a big storm brewing.

Yes, it's high time we got back to the house.

WOOOUIHHH

My hat! ... Hey! ... My hat!

Thundering typhoons! My very best hat!

BRROM

Ugh! Here comes the rain.

Good old Nestor! He's come to meet us with an umbrella.

Thank you, Nestor. We'd have been absolutely soaked.

By the whiskers of Kûrvi-Tasch! Someone else is watching them already.

Well, we're home again . . . and none too soon, either!

The telephone, Nestor.

RRIIING

Hello? . . . No Madam, I am not Mr Cutts the butcher! . . . No, Madam . . . NO, Madam! . . . Fiddle-de-dee, Madam!

. . . That's at least the twentieth time . . .

Quite so, Nestor. But one must always keep one's temper . . . especially with a lady . . . And besides, Nestor, you should never telephone during a storm: it is extremely dangerous.

That's that. And now, my friend, I think I'll just have a quiet drink, if you don't mind.

CRACK

Blistering barnacles! That flash of lightning wasn't far away.

In fact, I . . .

GLING BLING CLING

? !

Look at that!

?

The funny thing is, that happened AFTER the clap of thunder.

RRING RRING

Hello? . . . What? . . . Lamb chops?! . . . No, Madam, I am not Mr Cutts the butcher! And what's more Madam, it is highly dangerous to telephone during a storm. You should know better! And the best of luck, Madam!

CRACK

BANG

?

What shall I do, sir? Shall I . . . Shall I open it?

Yes, Nestor.

Ah! At last!

Hey! You there . . . Who d'you think you are?

Billions of blue blistering barnacles! That's a fine way to introduce yourself. And what d'you want here, anyway?

That's a long story, old boy . . .

Ah, the lights!

Yes, quite a story . . . I was driving along when, crack! . . . my windscreen shattered, and all the other windows as well. In that downpour too! So I said to myself: "Jolyon," (that's my name), Jolyon Wagg, of the Rock Bottom Insurance . . .

How nice! . . .

"Jolyon," I said to myself, "what are you going to do now? ". . . Then I saw your house. "I'll shelter there," I said . . . Here, take my coat, old chap.

You'd better stay here till the rain stops.

Nice little place you've got here. Must say I prefer something more modern, but still . . .

Oho! had a tiff with the wife, eh?

I . . . it was probably the lightning.

Lightning? . . . Ha! ha! ha! And I'll bet you weren't insured, eh, you old rascal? Well what a bit of luck that Jolyon Wagg dropped in: he'll soon fix you up with a neat little policy.

How kind.

Is that whisky you're drinking? You can pour one for me while you're about it. Not that I like the stuff: I'm just thirsty, that's all.

Not bad armchairs, these. I don't stand on ceremony, you know. A bit of a clown, that's me. Never a dull moment with me around, you bet!

I take after my Uncle Anatole; he was a barber, you know. Oh, you should have met him! A proper caution, he was. Always telling stories, make you die of laughing . . . Like this one . . . There were two men in a railway carriage, see . . .

Cheers!

CLING

They came from outside.

There's someone coming . . . Oh, it's Professor Calculus, on the way back from his laboratory.

Did you hear those shots?

No, it's over now. The rain has stopped.

Professor, just look at your hat! Excuse me . . .

Look! A bullet has gone right through it!

Oh! See! . . . a hole!

I can't understand it at all. The moths never used to make such big holes as these.

Quick, Captain. Let's have a look round the park.

Right. Just let me fetch a torch, and I'll be with you.

Calculus certainly came along this path . . .

Captain! Snowy's picked up a scent. Come on, let's follow him.

Oh! Look there!

Wooah!

Blistering barnacles! Do you think he's . . .

No: he's alive. His heart's beating . . . faintly . . .

We must send for the police at once.

You stay here while I go and telephone.

Blistering barnacles, what an evening! What an evening!

Oh, sir! . . . Sir! Something terrible's happened!

In heaven's name, what's the matter now?

Oh, sir! Your beautiful Venetian chandelier, upstairs. Smashed to smithereens, sir!

Later, Nestor, tell me later.

Hello? . . . Police station? . . . This is Marlinspike . . . What? You're Mr Cutts, the butcher?! Blistering barnacles! I . . . I beg your pardon. Wrong number.

I'm sure the number's 412 . . .

RRRING
RRRING

Hello? . . . What? No, Madam, I am not Mr Cutts the butcher! . . . No Madam! . . . No Madam! . . . Fiddle-de-dee, Madam!

SLAM

421

Marlinspike Police Station . . . Who is that? . . . Oh yes, Captain . . . Yes . . . Shots you say? Someone injured, in the grounds? Very good, Captain, we'll be with you right away.

. . . and another vase, sir . . .

Later, Nestor, later.

Oh, you've come back?

To fetch some water. The poor fellow wants a drink.

He talks with a strong foreign accent . . . He seems to be badly hurt.

Here we are. You'll soon see . . .

!

Great snakes! The wounded man . . . he's vanished!

I say . . . are you sure this is the place?

Absolutely certain. Look, the grass is flattened down!

WOOAH
WOOAH

WOOAH

OH!

!

Blistering barnacles! Come out of there, or I'll shoot!

Mercy! Have pity! Please don't kill me! I wouldn't harm a fly . . . I'm just a simple fellow . . .

Blistering barnacles, you don't have to tell me that! Just explain what you're doing down there!

Me? . . . I . . . I was hiding.

Somebody tried to murder me! I was walking towards my car . . . then suddenly: Bang! Bang! . . . So I said to myself, I said, "Jolyon, someone's trying to kill you . . ."

Wait . . . I can hear a car. It must be the police.

Are you the one who telephoned? . . . Good. The doctor and the ambulance are just behind us. Where is the casualty?

Here I am, Mr Inspector . . . Jolyon Wagg . . . That's me . . .

You've been shot?

Me? No.

But didn't you report that you'd found a wounded man?

Well, we did, but now he's vanished.

Then why were you pretending to be the victim?

But I am, Mr Inspector; I'm the victim of an attack; I was shot at. So I said to myself, "Jolyon," I said . . .

They weren't firing at him, sergeant, but the shots must have whistled past him. In fact one went through Calculus's hat.

And who, pray, is Calculus?

Calculus? He's a friend of mine. He came back to the hole with a house in his hat . . . No, I mean . . . Anyway, Tintin told me . . .

And who is Tintin?

Tintin? But this is Tintin! Here . . .

Hey, now where's he gone?

Go on, Snowy! Seek it out!

The wounded man got away through this hole in the hedge.

You've lost the scent, eh Snowy? I can guess why.

He was picked up by a car waiting here for him. There's nothing to be done. Come on, let's go back to the others.

. . . You mean the glass just broke by itself?

By itself, yes sergeant! And then . . .

Where have you sprung from?

Snowy picked up a scent. But it didn't lead anywhere.

There's nothing more we can do here. We'd better go back to the house; we can talk things over more easily there.

Yes, this case looks a hopeless muddle to me.

Next morning . . .

. . . TIN . . . BLOP . . . BLUB . . . PLOB

Blub... blub... blub...

Why? What's up, Captain?

There... in the... Blub...

Wait a minute. Rinse your mouth out first. I'll bring you a glass of water.

Hey, Snowy, be quiet. What are you howling for?

CLING

You... you... blub... you see! We're, we're bewitched, I tell you... We're bewitched!

And an hour later

Blistering barnacles, I don't know about you Tintin, but all this carry-on is beginning to get on my nerves.

Yes, ever since yesterday there's been a strange feeling about the house.

YOW-OW-OW... YOW-OW-OOOW...

? ?

ZZIING

Let's go and see. That sounded like a smash on the road.

? !

MILCO

5431 P

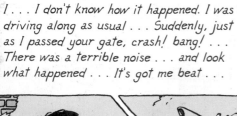

I... I don't know how it happened. I was driving along as usual... Suddenly, just as I passed your gate, crash! bang!... There was a terrible noise... and look what happened... It's got me beat...

Well, what do you make of it? It's exactly what happened to that creature, Jolyon Wagg.

It's fantastic.

TSSI.J.J.J.J.J.J.J

Look out!

Road-hog! Steam-roller! . . . Bully! . . . Dipsomaniac! . . . Nitwit!

Thomson and Thompson!!

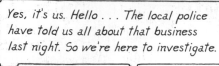
Yes, it's us. Hello . . . The local police have told us all about that business last night. So we're here to investigate.

To be precise: we're here.

At the right moment, too!

Just take a look here. This good fellow was driving quietly along past the front of the house when, CRACK . . . You see what happened? . . . What do you make of it?

The whole thing began last night . . .

Why, here comes our friend Calculus.

Hello, Cuthbert. Are you going away?

No, no. I'm just going away.

I'm flying to Geneva, where I'm taking part in a congress on nuclear physics.

To Geneva? . . . But you never mentioned it to me before.

No, not for very long: only two or three days. I must go now; I've just got time to catch the 11:42 train. Goodbye.

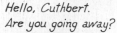

Well, that's one person who's quite unconcerned by all this business.

Yes, but somehow he seems rather more preoccupied than usual.

Look out! Here he comes! Get the chloroform ready.

'Morning Professor. Going to the village? . . . Yes? . . . Well, jump in.

By the whiskers of Kûrvi-Tasch! We've missed him!

Meanwhile . . .

. . . And that's the whole story, gentlemen. Can you make anything of it? . . . I just give up.

Hmm . . . We'll have to think this over.

All right. But there's just one thing: please don't gossip about this business. I don't want a whole crowd of sightseers here.

You can rely on us; "Mum's the word". That's our motto.

Yes, "Dumb's the word". That's our motto.

Good; thanks.

Next morning . . .

EL POPOLO
New York News
. . . AND NOW GLASSNIKS?
GRANDE PANIC
ÑOR HADDOCK
Daily Reporter
MYSTERY AT MARLINSPIK
Famous Sailor in Glass Sensation
ON DIMANCHE
Mystère du verre brisé
HAMBURGER TAGEBL
WAS IST LOS IN MARLINSPIKE?

Just look at that horde of rubber-necks! They can hardly wait to see the rest of my windows smashed to bits!

No doubt. But somehow I think they are going to be disappointed.

What do you mean?

It's just a thought . . . By the way, I know Calculus hates anyone going into his laboratory, but I'd rather like to have a look round in there. Have you got his key?

Yes . . . but what's the idea?

Well, I've been thinking about this business, and one thing struck me; the glass-breaking only occurred when Calculus was out; or, to be more accurate, when he was in his laboratory. And since he left for Geneva yesterday, nothing more has happened.

In a nutshell, you suggest our friend Cuthbert's responsible for all those incidents? But that's ridiculous!

I'm not suggesting anything, Captain. I'm simply trying to work it out.

Sniff . . . sniff . . .

I say, Captain, can you smell anything?

Sniff . . . Sniff . . .

It's just . . . sniff . . . tobacco, that's all.

Yes, but Calculus doesn't smoke.

Blistering barnacles, that's quite right!

Ha! ha! ha! ha! . . . Fooled you properly that time, didn't I, my hearties?

I . . . You . . . Billions of blue blistering barnacles! . . . I'll . . .

Ha! ha! . . . "Hands up!" . . . the old gag never fails!

Now then, this'll cheer you up: I've brought your insurance proposal.

!

I say, Captain, look what's written here in pencil, on this cigarette packet.

What is it?

Geneva
Hotel Cornavin

By thunder, that's the hotel in Geneva where Cuthbert usually stays.

Exactly.

Captain, something tells me the Professor's in danger there in Geneva. I'm going over to join him.

Cursh it! Whereshat paper got itshelf to?

And I suppose you think I'll let you go alone. Nonsense! I'm coming with you!

Right.

Here it ish!

Come on! To Geneva!

And the same day . . .

Hello . . . Hotel Cornavin? . . . Herr Szhrinkoff, please . . . Thank you . . . Hello, Stefan? . . . Yes, it's me . . . Look, you'd better get a move on. His friends have just left by air for Geneva.

3.30 p.m., at Cointrin Airport, Geneva . . .

OK, I get it: if they're here, we buzz off to Geneva and wait for them at Cornavin Station, at the Swissair bus terminal.

Three-quarters of an hour later, at Cornavin Station . . .

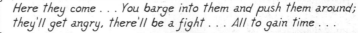

Here they come . . . You barge into them and push them around; they'll get angry, there'll be a fight . . . All to gain time . . .

Bah! Foiled! A gendarme . . .

Ah, there's a gendarme. We'll ask him.

Hotel Cornavin? You'll find it just across the road.

Thank you.

Is Professor Calculus staying here, please?

Professor Calculus? Yes, sir. His key is not on the board, so he must be in his room.

Phew, what a relief! Please tell him Captain Haddock and Tintin are here.

Certainly, sir.

What's up?

It's very odd . . . he isn't answering. Yet he should be in his room.

Perhaps he can't hear. We'd better go up. What number is his room, please?

Number 122, fourth floor. The lift is on your left.

Thank you. We'll leave our luggage here.

Fourth floor, please.

Certainly, sir.

Blistering barnacles, I know he's deaf . . . but all the same . . .

Supposing he's not in his room; supposing something's happened to him . . .

Not in his room, sir? Then his key should be here.

Great snakes! But there it is!

You're right . . . He must have gone out while my back was turned . . . I'm terribly sorry, sir.

You don't know where he might have gone?

Wait . . . I've got it. This morning Professor Calculus asked me for the time of trains to Nyon. I remember now: he said he'd take the 4:40. If you hurry you'll still catch him at the station.

Good. Thank you.

Look out! Here they come.

We have exactly seven minutes.

Hey, you! Why can't you watch where you're going?!

You clumsy oaf, are you suggesting it was my fault?

What?! You have a nerve, insulting me, you blundering bargee!

Captain!

Me, a bargee!! Billions of blue blistering barnacles, I'd have you know . . .

Floundering about! You ought to be locked up!

Please Captain, please! We shall miss Calculus . . .

Lucky for you I'm in a hurry!

Ha! ha! He says he's in a hurry!

Yes, in a hurry, you ectoplasmic by-product! Otherwise . . .

What happened? . . . I forgot it was a revolving door, that's all . . . and I pushed rather hard.

Let's hope we'll be in time.

Carpathian caterpillar! Just wait till I see him again!

The train to Nyon? . . . You're too late, sir; look, it's just gone.

Billions of blue blistering barnacles! All because of that Balkan beetle . . . I can't think why I don't go back . . .

That's a good idea; we'll go back.

I'm going to have a few words with that . . .

No you won't! We've other things to attend to.

Did Professor Calculus make any telephone calls after his arrival? . . . One moment, please; I'll inquire.

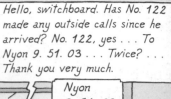

Hello, switchboard. Has No. 122 made any outside calls since he arrived? No. 122, yes . . . To Nyon 9. 51. 03 . . . Twice? . . . Thank you very much.

Nyon 9. 51. 03.

Hello, inquiries? Could you please give me the name and address of the subscriber at Nyon 9. 51. 03. Yes, I'll hold on . . .

Hello, yes . . . Topolino, Alfredo . . . 57 A, route de Saint-Cergue, Nyon . . . Thank you very much.

Could you take us to Nyon? 57 A, route de Saint-Cergue.

OK, sir.

Did you notice, Captain, that the chap we surprised in Calculus's laboratory and the one who tripped you up were wearing the same sort of raincoat?

Maybe . . .

Go on, Stefan. Overtake them!

Good. Now then, a little swerve, and jam on the brakes . . . hard!

Wham!

?

Crumbs! . . . What's happening? . . . We're skidding . . .

HELP! . . . HELP! . . . HELP!

Look! One's just come up again.
And there's a boy, too!

The driver? ... And Snowy?
Don't know. Didn't see.

BLUB BLUB

And Snowy?
No sign.

BLUB BLUB

WOOAH

Swan's dinner! I ask you!

I saw it all! The roadhogs! They swerved deliberately. If they'd wanted to push you into the lake they couldn't have done it better.
Ah, the driver's just come round.

Thank goodness ... Look here, there's something I must ask you to do for me. Would someone please take us on to Nyon? It's terribly urgent. We'll leave our names with you, to give to the police.

Half an hour later ...
Nyon

Here we are, gentlemen. This is Nyon. To reach route de Saint-Cergue you go through the tunnel and turn right.
Good. Thank you very much.

Here we are.

By the whiskers of Kûrvi-Tasch! It's them! ... They escaped! Run them down, Stefan: and this time, don't miss!

BANG
CLING
BONG

CLANG CLANG

Sssh!

?

CLANG
CLANG

Who are you?

Who am I? Sapristi! I'm Professor Topolino!

Yes, Professor Topolino. I've been brutally assaulted and thrown into the cellar! . . . Just wait till I see that monster Calculus again!

Calculus, a monster?!

Yes, Calculus! Do you know the scoundrel?

Sir, Calculus is our best friend, and I refuse to allow . . .

Oh, so he's a friend of yours. My heartiest congratulations! What delightful people you know. Anyway, who are you and what are you doing in my house?

Yes, we owe you an explanation. But shall we do that upstairs, when you have cleaned up a bit?

A quarter of an hour later . . .

To sum up. Last Thursday the first windows and glasses were broken.

And it's no joke. Imagine: you're holding a glass in your hand and suddenly . . . .

Just a minute, Captain . . . On the same day we heard the shots in the park, and found a wounded man who vanished. The next day Calculus left for Geneva, and the glass-breaking stopped immediately.

The day after that, a masked man slipped through our fingers in Calculus's laboratory, leaving behind a cigarette packet. On this packet was written: Geneva, Hotel Cornavin. We were anxious for our friend's safety, so we set off for Geneva.

Yes, without even stopping for a drink . . .

At the Hotel Cornavin, we had a row with a strange man. On the way from Geneva, a black Citroen tipped us into the lake.

We had a drink there, all right! But not as good as your excellent Swiss wine!

Finally, just near here, the same black Citroen tried to run us down, and missed by inches. A few minutes later, we found you in your cellar.

Er . . . That coal dust made me dreadfully thirsty. . . . What about you?

As for the packet of cigarettes, do you know this brand?

The brand that Boris smokes!

OOOH!

Who is Boris?

Boris? He's my servant. He smokes very little, and only those cigarettes. He gets them direct from Borduria.

From Borduria? . . . Boris is a Bordurian? . . . Where is he?

He left for home yesterday evening. They sent a telegram. His mother has just been taken ill.

Oho! It's '53!

I think I'm beginning to understand. Yes . . . But what's your story, Professor?

Well, it's like this. About a month ago I had the first letter from Calculus.

Your wine has rare distinction.

He wrote to say that he was on the verge of a sensational discovery, in the field of ultrasonics. As I am a specialist in that subject, he sought my advice. Last week another letter arrived . . . He had succeeded.

But it seems that the consequences of his invention so alarmed him that he wished to talk to me. I arranged to see him today.

Er . . . This bottle was intended for him?

Exactly. But help yourself if you feel like it. . . . This afternoon Calculus arrived, a little earlier than I expected, and we began to chat . . .

Then I bent down to pick up some papers. I looked up, and there was Calculus, brandishing a cosh . . . Then I came to in the cellar, bound and gagged.

I've got it!

Oh, sorry! . . .

Not at all!

Do you know this man?

Never seen him. Who is he?

Calculus! The one and only Calculus! So it wasn't he who knocked you out; it was someone else, masquerading as the Professor. Meanwhile the real Calculus arrived . . .

You're sure the timing mechanism hasn't stopped?

Don't panic! Only a few seconds to go . . .

And Calculus did come here; his umbrella proves that . . . He was met by the man who knocked you out, and then pretended to be you.

Good health, Professor!

That's how it must have happened . . .

BOOOM

Up she goes! That's got rid of the whole bunch at one stroke!

A few minutes later...

DING-GLING-GLING-GLING

Help! Help! We're under here!

Are you hurt?

Don't know... Don't think so... But be careful.

There's enough damage been done already, without smashing this bottle!

But hurry up! There were three of us in the house, and a dog.

There!... Glug... Glug...

That's it... Now I can pass out!

Ah, here come the others.... Injured?

They're all unconscious.

Were there any casualties?

Three; two looked in very bad shape.

Next morning...

...Topolino were taken from the wreckage. Fragments of a bomb were found in the debris and foul play is suspected. The police have detained two men found loitering in the vicinity of the crime, questioning passers-by. These two men will appear before the examining magistrate this morning.

Meanwhile speculation is rife as to the motive behind this attack, and every effort is being made to discover why Professor Topolino's house should

Bring in the two men, sergeant.

Very good, sir.

Look at this cigarette, Captain. The same brand . . . once again!

Thundering typhoons, you're right.

. . . It was a C.D. car . . . Diplomatic Corps. That means from an embassy, and most probably the Bordurian Embassy . . . We must find out where that is. A post office directory will tell us. We'd better go back to Nyon.

There . . . Bordurian Embassy, "Les Cygnes", Rolle.

Rolle . . . That's a few miles from Nyon.

Well then, this afternoon we'll reconnoitre. We'll go out to Rolle and spy out the land; and tonight, Captain, we'll go into action!

That night . . .

PCHH

PCHH

Blood-suckers!

Man-eating pests!

PCHH

PCHH

Lucky I brought this along!

Don't make a sound Captain, we're nearly there.

PCHH

PCHH

BZZZ BZZZ BZZZ

Wait, just a few more shots!

PCHH

BZZRRBZR

Here comes an absolute whopper! Listen to the din!

PCHH

OH! . . . Sorry!

He's landing on the lawn . . . Moor the boat and we'll have a look.

Look over there; someone's coming.

Crumbs! The man in the middle . . . no mistaking that silhouette . . . It's Calculus! They're going to put him aboard the helicopter!

Good heavens! What's happening?

Someone's trying to rescue Calculus! Quick, Captain, let's give them a hand!

I'm with you! Come on!

...But how can we tell friends from enemies?

Go for the ugliest... That won't be difficult - you'll see.

Now which has the ugliest mug? It looks about fifty-fifty...

Tintin! Is it really you? I can't believe my eyes!

Next please!

It's the thug who knocked me out in Calculus's laboratory, back at Marlinspike ...the man with the cigarettes!

Quick, Captain, come on!

Rapp! ...Noh dzem bûthsz!

Half a mo'... I'm coming...

PCHH

My umbrella! ...My umbrella!

My umbrella!

The Captain... we must wait for the Captain...

Here I come!

The brutes! They've knocked out Tintin!

A pylon! Power cables!

We just missed them. But blistering barnacles, we're out of control!

Whew! We're safe!

I think we must have trimmed the treetops.

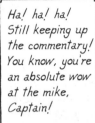

Ha! ha! ha! Still keeping up the commentary! You know, you're an absolute wow at the mike, Captain!

You prize purple jellyfish, you! Must I kill myself drumming it into your thick skull? This is no joke! . . . Now listen to me, Wagg . . .

Don't bother, Captain; it's too late anyway. Look: the petrol gauge is down to zero. A bullet must have holed the tank. The only thing we can do is to land on the road in front of the car and force it to stop.

Help!! She's misfiring!

PTTT
PTTT
PTTT

! !
?

No, the engine's picked up.

Quick! Down on the road!

That's it!

!

There they are! BUT . . . ?!

D 25
CERVENS
5,2 Km.

Thundering typhoons! They must have a Jack Brabham at the wheel!

That's that. They've slipped through our fingers . . . And Calculus with them.

Now what'll we do?

First we'd better clear the road, in case of accidents.

Then continue on foot . . . and try to hitch-hike.

Ah! A car . . . Let's thumb a lift.

Blackguards! . . . Egoists! . . . Nitwits! . . . Troglodytes! . . . Polygraphs! . . .

It's incredible what cads some drivers are. They see you like that, all alone on the road, and whoosh! . . . they sweep past! Blistering barnacles, what times we live in!

Hey, here comes another.

Beasts! . . . Autocrats! . . . Profiteers! . . . Fat faces! . . . Tramps! . . .

There ought to be a law to make those infernal mileage-merchants stop when people signal.

Ah, another. Let's try again.

Bah, they won't stop. You'll see.

I say, they've stopped.

TS!!!!

Oh well, we needn't despair. There are still a few gentlemen left in the world.

Tintin! . . . Wait! . . . STOP! . . .

?

Quick! Into the wood . . .

Hurry! . . . Get down: like me.

Why in that particular puddle?

SPLOSH

I say, Captain, what are you doing?

Blistering barnacles, get down! They'll start shooting any moment! Didn't you recognise the black Citroen?

The black Citroen? . . . No, Captain, you've got it wrong. It was black all right, but it had a French number plate: the other one was Swiss.

Are . . . are you quite sure?

Absolutely certain. Come on, perhaps they're still there.

But I promise you, my pet, there were two people in the road who signalled to me.

And I say, Jules, that it's time you went to the oculist and ordered stronger glasses.

And on top of it all, you're soaked . . .

Oh, the sun will soon dry me off.

Hmm! I wouldn't count on it.

If only we had an umbrella!

An umbrella? Captain, what idiots we are. Look!

?

...Yes, and meanwhile poor Calculus is being whisked further and further away!

At last! There's a tobacconist. I'm going to buy an ounce or two.

You go on. I won't be a minute.

TS!!!!

BANG

HELP!...

Oh goodness! How awful! Poor Captain! What a ghastly thing to happen!

Bandit!... Anthropophagus!... Steam-roller!... Highwayman!... Travelling at that speed! I suppose you want to break the sound-barrier? You thundering misguided missile, you!

Bashi-bazouk!... Ectoplasm!

Mamma mia! It was you!... Basta!... And now why you spitta all over my window?

Presto! Window-wash!

Eccolà!

Excuse me, sir, but could you please help us? We're chasing some car-bandits... they've kidnapped one of our friends, Professor Calculus, and...

Madonna!... Uno bandito... we chase? Va bene! You get in my car...

You in good?

OK.

SLAM

BRRROOM

Avanti!

Billions of blue blistering barnacles! Must you do that? Can't you start off like other people?

Scusi!

I show you... Italian car, Italian driver, the best in the world, no? Avanti! Prestissimo! We catcha him, il povero Professore!

Perhaps we'd better explain. Our friend Calculus has an invention which secret agents from a foreign power are trying to steal. That is why they kidnapped Calculus.

But a rival gang, probably secret agents from another country, grabbed our friend.

Hitch-hikers! Blistering barnacles, there ought to be a law against them!

As I was saying, this second gang snatched our friend from the first lot. We . . . er . . . Don't you think we'd better slow down?

DANGER WET TAR

Mamma mia! . . . Whatta is happening? This noise is peculiare. Diavolo! I think now: uno pistone? . . . Una valvola?

CLICK CLICK CLICK CLICK
CLICK CLICK
CLICK

It . . . it . . . it's nothing. . . . It . . . it . . . it's my . . . my t-t-t-teeth . . . ch-ch-ch-ch-chattering . . .

Olà! You think I drive troppo presto?

Er . . . I believe the Captain thinks that you're flying too low . . .

CLICK

?

Ten thousand thundering typhoons! Must you drive like a lunatic?

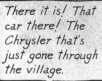

There it is! That car there! The Chrysler that's just gone through the village.

HELP! . . .

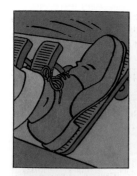

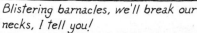

Blistering barnacles, we'll break our necks, I tell you!

There they are again!

Bene! Bene! We catcha them up!

Thundering typhoons! The level-crossing barrier's closing. We're too late to get through.

ZZINGG ZZINGG

Whew! Thundering typhoons, if we go on like this I'll have a heart attack!

. . . Now, we give a nice little swerve, so! . . .

. . . We put on the brakes, so! . . . Ecco! . . . Superbissimo!

That's odd. I can't see Calculus . . .

By heaven!! What d'you think you're playing at? What do you want?

What do we want? Quite simply: Calculus. Where is he?

Calculus? And what might that be: Calculus? A plant? An animal? A chemical?

You know as well as we do! What have you done with him?

I'd ask you to mind your manners. Once and for all, I've never heard of your Candyfloss! You can see that my chauffeur and I are alone in my car . . .

What about the boot?

Young man, I could say that the contents of my boot are none of your business: but since I don't wish to be nasty . . .

There! Now where's your Coelacanth? Inside the spare wheel, I suppose.

Does that satisfy you, Mr Sherlock Holmes? Or would you like to dismantle my carburettor? No? In that case, get out of the road and let me pass. You've wasted enough of my time already.

I...

But...

Mamma mia! You fool me nicely, yes? ... You tella me the big fib, yes? You just wanta to make hitch-hike ... and me stupido who believes you! Madonna, how you fool me! Va bene! Now you walk. Addio!

What can have happened? Did we follow the wrong car? ... Or did Calculus stay in the motor-boat? ...

GREAT SNAKES!

Hey, what's the matter? Now what's burning you up?

YEOW!

What idiots we are! Under the back seat!

Why? ... What? ... Which back seat?

It was rather high up ... That's where they've hidden poor Calculus! We let ourselves be hoodwinked like a couple of kids. Come on!

Old Calculus has certainly led us a pretty dance around the countryside!

That aeroplane looks as if it's landing. Is there an airfield near here? If that's the case, we're saved.

Come on, let's take this footpath. When we get to the airfield we'll ask if there's a plane available.

What's all this? ... No airfield? ... It's come down in a meadow.

Look! There, behind those trees!

The Chrysler!!

There's Calculus! They're putting him aboard the plane. Quick Captain!

By St. Vladimir! There are those madmen again!

Quick, Stanislas, climb aboard. And start up the engine, Boldoff; hurry! Too bad about the car: we'll abandon it.

Step on it, Boldoff!

Faster! Faster!

What are you waiting for? Take off!

Ah! That's it!

At last! Calculus is ours!

Wooah! Wooah!

WOOAH!

YOW! OW! OW!

HELP! HELP!

?

41

Hello! What's happened to you?

Er . . . nothing . . . a slight mishap. But read this; it's incredible.

BORDURO-SYLDAVIAN INCIDENT

Bordurian fighters force down Syldavian plane

"VIOLATION OF OUR AIR-SPACE"

SAYS SZOHÔD

A Bordurian Air Ministry communiqué reports that a Syldavian aircraft has been intercepted by fighters while flying over Bordurian territory. Despite repeated warnings, says the communiqué

"UNPROVOKED TASCHIST AGGRESSION"

KLOW PROTESTS

In an official note the Syldavian Ministry of Foreign Affairs has protested vigorously against "unprovoked aggression by the Bordurian Air Force towards an unarmed Syldavian passenger

Great snakes! This alters everything. I bet that's the plane Calculus was in. Now he's fallen into Bordurian hands again. They never give up, do they?

Your tickets for Klow, sir.

We don't need them! We're going to Szohôd, in Borduria.

Yes . . . er . . . Can we by any chance . . .

I'm sorry, sir, the flight to Szohôd is fully booked. The last two seats have just been taken. However, if you would care to wait . . .

. . . we may have a last-minute cancellation. In that case we can make arrangements for you.

By the whiskers of Kûrvi-Tasch! They want to go to Szohôd, you can bet your life. But we took the last two seats. I wonder . . .

You'll wait here? Good. I'm just going to see if I can get through to Marlinspike.

All right.

Yes, Marlinspike 421. Thank you, I'll hold on.

Hello? . . . Hello, Marlinspike? Hello, is that you, Nestor? . . . What? . . . Who's that speaking? . . .

Cutts the butcher speaking . . . What can I do for you? . . . Hello?

Hello, operator. That was the wrong number. I asked for 421 . . . Yes, 421.

Hello? Hello, is that 421? Is that you, Nestor? This is Captain Haddock. I . . . Who is that speaking? . . . Who?!

Wagg . . . Jolyon Wagg . . . Proper lark this is, eh? You old humbug, you didn't half give me a laugh with your helicopter chase . . . What? . . . What am I doing here?

It turned out nice, so I brought the wife for a little visit to your country seat . . . Yes . . . Who? . . . Nestor? . . . I'll hand you over to him; he's got a good joke to tell you . . . Hi, Nestor, it's your boss.

Hello . . . Ah, Nestor, how are you? . . . Yes . . . No . . . Perhaps . . . And what's your news at Marlinspike?

WHAT?

Right away, François.

Well done Snowy! He's been to fetch Calculus's umbrella.

Crumbs! This doesn't belong to Calculus. Snowy! Where in the world did you pinch this from?

Thundering typhoons! Quick, Tintin, hand me that brolly.

Hey, I think you've lost your umbrella! Here it is.

Hello, what's that on my nose?

Oh, it's the bit of sticking-plaster.

It's off now . . .

Thundering . . .

. . . typhoons!

!

?

Pardon me, but you have something on your hat.

A bit of sticking-plaster.

Now I wonder where that came from?

It's sticky! . . .

And it's stuck!

Oh,   bother it!

Ah,   it's gone.

Well, that's got rid of that!

At Cointrin airport, 1.40 p.m.

Here we go, on our way to Szohôd . . . I only hope we find poor Calculus there.

Billions of bilious blue blistering barnacles!

Just look at this confounded sticking-plaster! How did it get itself on to my cap? It's black magic, I tell you!

Meanwhile, in Geneva . . .

Hello, operator, I want Szohôd 322.18 . . . Yes, Szohôd . . . What? A delay? But it's urgent. I . . . Good. Try and hurry things along.

Hello? . . . Hello? . . . Yes, I can hear you . . . CRACKLE . . . FRRT . . . Hello, Szohôd? Hello, I . . . FRRT . . . Hello?

2.17 p.m.

2.35 p.m.

Hello? Yes, I can hear you . . . Hello? . . . GLOUIP . . . CRR . . . Will you . . . Hello? . . . What? . . . Ah, it's you, Szhrinkoff. Amaïh! . . . CRRR . . . Hello?

2.52 p.m.

3.03 p.m.

Hello? . . . FRRWT . . . Hello, I can't hear you CLACK . . . What? . . . FRRT . . . CRRACK . . . Can't you speak up?! . . . What?

3.48 p.m.

Yes, Haddock. A sort of sea-dog with a beard . . . CLACK . . . BZZ . . . Beard . . . HIIP . . . No, beard . . . GRR . . . He has a beard! . . . XWUUI . . . XWUUUI . . . Yes beard!

4.30 p.m.

SZOHÔD

Hello! CRACK . . . Yes, I've got it . . . CRACK . . . FRR-RRT . . . By the whiskers of Kûrvi-Tasch, what a line! . . . Captain Haddock and Tintin: OK, OK. I'll warn the airport control at once . . . Amaïh!

SZOHÔ
TZHÔL · DOUANE · CUS

Hello, airport police here . . . Amaïh Kûrvi-Tasch, sir! The plane from Geneva? It's just in . . . What? . . . What names?

AMAIH
XSZY-GL

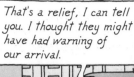
That's a relief, I can tell you. I thought they might have had warning of our arrival.

SZTÔPP!
?! ?!

You Captain Haddock? And you Tintin? . . . You come please. My officer want talk with you.

What? Who is this officer of yours?

Captain, wait. You've got something . . .

A few minutes later . . .

Ah, Captain, this is a great privilege for us. We in Borduria salute you, hero of that glorious interplanetary flight . . . Amaïh!

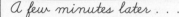

And you too, Mänhir Tintin. I am proud to shake the hand which . . . er . . . first set foot on the Moon. I salute you. Amaïh!

You . . . You're too kind.

The ancient traditions of Bordurian hospitality demand that we ensure your absolute comfort and safety.

Szplug! What is this?

As I was saying: your safety . . . Two interpreters will therefore accompany you during your stay here. They will take you wherever you may wish to go . . . and at whatever time.

These gentlemen, Krônick and Klûmsi, are entirely at your service . . . They will take you to the Hotel Zsnôrr, where rooms are booked for you. I wish you a pleasant stay . . . Amaïh!

Thanks . . . very much.

Ten minutes later, in Szohôd . . .

. . . And this is Kûrvi-Tasch Platz. Your hotel is just round the corner.

HOTEL ZSNÔRR
Here we are. This is it.

One moment, please. We'll see about your rooms.

Be careful! Those two ostrogoths in Geneva certainly tipped off the police here. We must keep our eyes open.

Oh! . . . Quick! . . . Hide! Hide!

BIANCA CASTAFIORE!!!

Did you see? That was Signora Bianca Castafiore, the Milanese nightingale. She's singing at the Szohôd Opera. If you wish, we will go to hear her one evening: she is sublime as Marguerite, in "Faust".

Oh yes . . .

Here are the keys. We will escort you to your rooms.

This is yours, Mänhir Captain. I hope you will be comfortable.

Yours is a little further down: unfortunately there were no adjoining rooms.

Here you are, Mänhir Tintin. We will come and fetch you for dinner, in an hour. If you need us before then, don't hesitate to ring: we're entirely at your service.

Thank you, gentlemen.

We're prisoners all right, Snowy, and no mistake about it. The fact that it's a gilded cage doesn't make any difference.

Golly! The lap of luxury!

RRING RRING

Hello? . . . Oh, it's you, Captain . . . What?

Blistering barnacles, I said that at the first opportunity we'll ditch those two coleoptera! That's agreed, isn't it?

I . . . er . . . Oh yes. You're referring to those two butterflies you caught by the lake, in Geneva. But those aren't coleoptera, Captain, they're lepidoptera.

What are you jabbering about? Lepidoptera? Lepidoptera to you, too! I . . . Hello? . . . Hello?

Crumbs! How can I make him understand that our telephone is bound to be tapped?

CLICK

RRING RRING

Hello? . . . Yes . . . Yes . . . We were cut off. I . . . er . . . Don't worry about the butterflies, Captain . . .

Let's talk about the simply wonderful hospitality of this exquisite country. What good taste! What tact! And then their . . . um . . . their courtesy. And above all their . . . how shall I put it? their friendliness. Friendliness which is entirely . . . er . . . friendly . . . Um . . .

You . . . But . . . What . . . Let . . . But . . . Look here . . . I . . . Blister . . . Thunder . . .

Keep on recording. This could be interesting.

Ten thousand thundering typhoons! . . . Now I'm going to chuck you out of the window!

What? . . . No, blistering barnacles! It's that thundering bit of sticking-plaster. It's following me about!

Well, good luck. I'll leave you to sort things out together. But don't forget, we go down to dinner in an hour.

An hour later . . .

Captain, I propose we crack a bottle of champagne in honour of these gentlemen.

Champagne?! Champagne for this gang?

OWW!

Oh, poor Captain! It must be your rheumatism. Well, there's nothing like champagne for curing that. Will you call the wine-waiter?

Gentlemen, a toast to Borduria and her glorious ruler, Marshal Kûrvi-Tasch!

Amaïh Kûrvi-Tasch!

Amaïh Kûrvi-Tasch!

An hour later . . .

I say, they're having quite a party at table seven. That's their fourth bottle!

Ha! ha! I'm no fool! . . . You want to make us tight . . . To find out where . . . hic . . . Professor Calculus is . . . Hic . . . But you won't learn a thing. We'll shut up like trams . . . No, like prams . . . like lambs . . . no, like clams . . .

Don't let's worry about Calculus. He'll have to shift for himself.

That's right! Hic . . . Don't let's worry. Anyway . . . hic . . . I don't know anything. Honestly . . . It's Sponsz . . . hic . . . the Chief of the "ZEP" . . . our secret pol . . . hic . . . he's the only one who knows . . . And Calculus . . .

Good . . . good. Let's forget silly old Calculus. It's time for bed.

Will you take us right up to our rooms?

Hic . . .

I . . . hic . . . I'll stay in the corridor.

Fine . . . Good idea!

OK. Mine's locked in your room.

And mine in yours.

THUMP THUMP THUMP THUMP

Thundering typhoons! He'll rouse the whole hotel.

Wait. I'll open the door and we'll see . . .

THUMP

Hic . . . Not gone to bed yet? . . . I just wanted . . . hic . . . to give you your cap . . . Hic . . . Now, I'll stay in the . . . hic . . . corridor. I'll be . . . hic . . . very comfortable; they've put a bed there.

112 BANG

That's it! . . . Now then, let's go . . .

Crumbs! Get back, quick!

?

Get inside! And hurry!

Disgustingly drunk . . . That's why I telephoned the ZEP immediately.

You did well. All the exits are guarded.

Whew! They've gone.

Did you hear?

Wait. Perhaps over here . . .

Saved! It's the fire-escape!

Blistering barnacles! We're trapped!

What'll we do? . . . Ah, I think I've got an idea.

All right, Captain! . . . Ready?

HOTEL ZSNÔRR
ZSERVIZ

BANG

This is it! . . . Come on!

A broken light-bulb! But where can that have come from?

HI!!

SZTÔPP!

Quick! The lights are still green!

Meanwhile . . .

Yes gentlemen, we of the High Command are assembled today to hear about a remarkable discovery. After protracted research, Bordurian scientists have succeeded in perfecting a weapon . . .

. . . that will soon make H-bombs and ballistic missiles as obsolete as pikes and muskets! . . . The day is not far off, gentlemen, when this weapon will make the people of Borduria, and their glorious ruler Kûrvi-Tasch, masters of the world . . . To prove this to you, I invite you to give your undivided attention to this screen.

Here, challenging the world with its gigantic skyscrapers, is a great trans-Atlantic city, which it is superfluous to name.

Gentlemen, at our command, this city is doomed. In a few seconds it will be reduced to rubble. I have only to press this button . . .

So!

You see those proud buildings swaying on their foundations; they are cracking, disintegrating, toppling . . .

. . . and crumbling to dust. A whole city is wiped from the face of the earth!

Extraordinary!

Splendid!

Amazing!

We must keep calm, gentlemen! And above all, we must be patient. The great city which you saw disintegrating before your eyes was, for the time being, no more than . . .

. . . this model of glass and china . . . Yes, I can see the bitter disappointment on your faces: you are sorry not to have witnessed the actual destruction of a real city! Have faith, gentlemen!

This miniature city was destroyed from a distance by the machine you see here. It is an ultrasonic instrument. Up to now it is only effective against glass and china . . .

But in the near future we shall be able to destroy AT LONG RANGE not only glass and china, but bricks, concrete, and steel! The designs for this tremendous weapon already exist: that is all I can tell you at the moment . . . But when our hour strikes . . .

. . . then the enemies of Borduria will be stricken with terror before the might of our annihilating power . . .

Colonel, sir. You are wanted on the telephone.

Hello, Colonel Sponsz speaking . . . Oh, it's you Laszlo . . . What? . . . They've vanished! By the whiskers of Kûrvi-Tasch, it's impossible!

You lost track of them somewhere near the Opera? . . . Area surrounded? . . . Good . . . Well, as soon as I've finished here I'll trot along to the Opera and check the security precautions. And while I'm about it, I'll go and hear Castafiore.

An hour later, at the Szohôd Opera House . . .

Captain! . . . Wake up, Captain! It's the interval . . . Captain! . . .

You see, this is the safest place for us . . . No one could possibly guess that we'd taken refuge at the Opera!

It's true, Captain. When you're in a crowd there's always less chance of being noticed.

52

Just look, there's Colonel Sponsz, the Chief of Police.

So it is . . . Colonel Sponsz!

Sponsz, here! . . . And Calculus's fate depends on that man! Little does he know that he and his two henchmen passed within a yard of us!

RRRRRRRRRING

It's the end of the interval. Shall we push off? . . .

I think it's better to wait till the end of the show. Then we can leave with the crowd.

An hour later . . .

It's hopeless! . . . The exits are stiff with policemen. Let's try to slip out through the stage door.

Why, look who's here! It's Tintin!

18

Hello, my dear young friend. How delightful to see you here.

Aha, you little flatterer, so you've come to congratulate me, with this . . . this fisherman . . . Mr? . . . Mr? . . .

Er . . . Hoddack . . . er . . . Haddad . . . Excuse me, Haddock.

Come into my dressing-room . . . Yes, yes . . . I can't leave my admirers in the passage . . . I've put on Marguerite's prettiest gown for you . . . Come along in.

You heard it? . . . Such a success, wasn't it? . . . One of the greatest triumphs of my career . . . What applause . . . especially for the Jewel Song . . . They were in ecstasies, weren't they, Mr Paddock?

Haddock, Mad . . . !

RAT TAT TAT

Again? Ah, they won't leave me alone for a moment! . . . Oh well . . . Come in!

Signora, it's Colonel Sponsz, the Chief of Police. He wishes to pay his respects to you.

But of course! Show him in, girl . . .

? ?

Just a minute, Signora! . . . The Colonel . . . Listen, I'll explain everything later . . . but at all costs he mustn't find us here!

Dio! . . . What shall we do?

Irma, wait a moment! . . . Quick! Hide in my wardrobe, behind this curtain.

There . . . Show the Colonel in, Irmaa ♫ . . .

I am deeply honoured, Ma'am to . . . to find myself in the presence of the celebrated singer who . . . er . . . who . . .

Fie, Colonel! You make me blush!

But do please sit down.

You are too kind . . .

Oh, forgive me! . . . I've sat on something . . . It's a naval officer's cap . . .

Blistering barnacles! My cap!

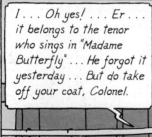
I . . . Oh yes! . . . Er . . . it belongs to the tenor who sings in "Madame Butterfly" . . . He forgot it yesterday . . . But do take off your coat, Colonel.

With pleasure, Ma'am.

Take the Colonel's coat, please, Irmaa ♫ . . .

Now Irma, bring the champagne . . . It's an old habit of mine, Colonel: champagne after each performance. You'll take a glass with me?

I fear I intrude, Ma'am.

Not at all, not at all. Come, Colonel, make yourself useful . . . You may open the bottle.

But of course, Ma'am. Your wish is my command.

RAT TAT TAT

Come in.

Oh! Excuse me, Colonel . . . I . . . We were ordered to search the Opera House from top to bottom . . . For those two foreigners . . .

Is that so?

I suppose you think you'll find them in here, you dunderheaded nitwits! Go on, get out! About turn, before I explode!

POP

Please excuse those numskulls, Ma'am. They're hunting for two spies . . .

Oh, do tell me about them, Colonel, I adore spy-stories! . . . Your health, Colonel.

Spies! Us! Barefaced liar.

Your health, Ma'am . . . Well, it's this way: our secret service have managed to . . . to "invite" to Borduria a foreign professor, originator of a sensational discovery. It concerns a secret weapon. Once this has been perfected, it will give us world supremacy.

Oh, but that's simply wonderful!

Yes, but the perfecting of it depends upon the professor. And up till now he refuses to give us his detailed drawings. His reason: he doesn't want his invention used for warlike purposes . . . I ask you!

These Professors! Always wanting the moon!

Ha! ha! You don't know how true that is! But just now he's on the earth! Between ourselves, he's in the fortress of Bakhine. And by the whiskers of Kûrvi-Tasch, he'll stay there till he decides to give up the plans!

Oh, I'm sure he will in the end.

I hope so, for his sake! Anyway, I have a signed order for his release in my coat pocket. Tomorrow he'll have to choose: either he gives up his plans, or he'll never be heard of again.

And supposing he does give up his plans, Colonel. What happens when he gets home, and tells all?

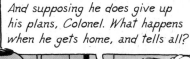

Ha! ha! I've foreseen that. If we set the professor free, it will be in the presence of two representatives of the International Red Cross. He'll have to declare in front of them that he came to Borduria of his own free will, to offer us his plans . . . I have passes for these two representatives in my coat, too.

How clever of you, Colonel! . . . Brilliant!

Oh, just part of my job, Ma'am . . . But I am gossiping, and time passes . . . If I may dare to presume . . . My wife is giving a small party for some friends tonight . . . and it would give us much pleasure if you would agree to come, just as you are, and sing for us.

But of course . . . Irmaa ♫ . . . The Colonel's coat please, and mine.

Next morning, at the fortress of Bakhine . . .

I see. Colonel Sponsz has sent you to take charge of the professor. Your papers look in order to me, and the order of release . . . However . . .

. . . Better safe than sorry. I'd better check that everything's all right. Will you excuse me? . . .

But . . . but of course!

D-d-do!

Hello, ZEP? . . . This is the commandant at Bakhine, Major Kardouk. Would you put me through to Colonel Sponsz?

Hello? . . . What? . . . Oh, he's not in yet . . . Who is that? . . . His secretary? . . . In that case, perhaps you can help me . . .

Oh yes. Two representatives from the International Red Cross . . . Their passes? Quite all right, Major, I made them out myself. And the order for release? Yes, Major, that's quite all right too; the colonel signed it yesterday morning. Yes. Amaïh!

Well, gentlemen, everything's perfectly in order. I'll send for Professor Calculus.

A moment later . . .

Ah! The joy . . . popom-pom . . . pompity pom . . . pom

Here comes the chief. He sounds in good form this morning.

Amaïh! Kavitch . . . What's the news? . . . Any trace of Calculus's friends?

Nothing at all, Colonel. Not a sign of them.

That's tiresome . . . Very tiresome. I wonder where those two artful dodgers managed to hide . . . Nothing else, besides that?

Nothing at all, sir.

Oh yes . . . Major Kardouk rang up.

Kardouk? That old bore! And what did he want this time?

He wanted to know if the order you signed releasing Professor Calculus was official.

By the whiskers of Kûrvi-Tasch! When a document bears my signature, is it or is it not official?

Yes, Colonel. That's exactly what I told him, sir . . .

You . . . you did say the order releasing Professor Calculus?

Why . . . yes, Colonel . . .

?

!

The papers! . . . It's treason! . . . They've been stolen!

RRRING

Hello! . . . Yes, it's me . . . Amaïh! Colo . . . What? . . . Professor Calcu . . . But sir, I . . .

WHAT? . . . Their car's just gone? By all the hairs in the whiskers of Kûrvi-Tasch, if you don't get them back . . . I'll have you shot!

Yes, it's me, Haddock! . . . And there's Tintin, driving us to safety.

I'll tell you the whole story. The biggest joke is that Colonel Sponsz himself provided the means of your escape! . . . Magnificent, eh? And luckily it all happened at the Opera House; it only took a jiffy to find all we needed for disguises! Quite something, eh?

And my umbrella?

Yes, but don't start counting your chickens . . . It's two hours by car to the frontier, and if our little bluff is discovered before we're across . . .

CRACK
CRACK

What did I tell you? Motor bikes!

They've raised the alarm! That's bad . . .

Quick, Captain. Unclip the hood at the back. When you've done that, I'll let go at the front . . .

One!

Two! They're both down in the daisies!

Now, Captain; we were talking about my umbrella . . .

Saved for the moment; but I've a feeling that was only the first round . . .

OH! . . . How right I was! . . . Look there, a tank blocking the road! . . . Jam on the brakes!

We're skidding!

HELP! . . . HELP!

By the whiskers of Kûrvi-Tasch, they came a cropper!

If they're underneath that lot, there's not very   much to be done . . .

BROOMM

A chance in a million! If we hadn't been thrown clear of the car . . .

Poor old Calculus is fearfully groggy . . . I say, Tintin, watch out! You'll have us in the ditch again!

I'm doing my best, but . . .

. . . I haven't driven a tank since our Moon trip.

Crumbs! . . . A road-block!

Too bad! I'll ram it.

What? . . . What's that you say? . . . A tank? . . . They've taken a tank!! Blow them up! . . . Exterminate them! . . . Pulverise them!! . . . I . . .

Trying to stop us with that kind of ramshackle erection!

Look out, here they come! . . . Don't miss! . . . FIRE!

I always told you this make of gun could be improved.

Hooray! He's coming round at last. Cuthbert! Cuthbert! It's me, old fellow . . . We're safe . . .

Ooh!

My umbrella! Have you got my umbrella?

Blistering barnacles, your umbrella! This is a fine time to worry about an umbrella!

Nonsense Captain! I'm talking about my umbrella. Surely you can't have lost it?

All right, I have lost your brolly . . . in Geneva, if you want to know.

That's good. I was hoping you hadn't lost it . . . You see, I hid my drawing . . .

Drawing? . . .

Boring? Of course it's not boring. I'm talking about the detailed drawings of my ultrasonic instrument, on microfilm. I hid them in the handle of my umbrella . . . So you see, if you'd lost it . . .

Hey!

I . . . What are all those things in the road?

MINES!

Too late! We can't stop in time! We'll blow up! HELP! . . . HELP! . . . HELP! . . .

By the whiskers of Kûrvi-Tasch! Who unloaded all that dud stuff on me? . . . It's sabotage!

Mines? . . . What are you jabbering about? We would have blown up. And talking of blowing up, I hope these things aren't dangerous. There's a case under my seat . . .

Those?

They're thunderflashes . . . used on exercises. When you light them, they explode with a terrific bang . . . Great snakes, it can't be true!

The frontier! We're coming to the frontier!

TZHÔL

Crumbs! . . . We're cornered this time!

59

A barricade! . . . With anti-tank defences on both sides! What shall we do?

Only one weak spot: the customs house itself! Here we go!

TZHÔL

HÔL

We're safe, Cuthbert!

Safe!

At last! Now I can have a quiet smoke to celebrate . . . the first since we set off.

The other frontier post. Nothing can happen to us now.

BOOOM

They must be refugees from the Kûrvi-Tasch regime . . . Poor devils! They'll be blown to bits.

Blistering typhoons! . . . I . . . I forgot all about them . . . those thundering thunder-things . . .

Two days later, in Geneva . . .

An umbrella, you say? Er . . . what sort of umbrella?

LOST PROPERTY

CRASH BANG CLANG BOOM

Snowy! Here, Snowy!

My umbrella! My own little umbrella! At last I've found you!

And now watch carefully . . . I grasp the handle . . . I unscrew it . . . There . . . And hey-presto, what do we see? . . .

My plans!?!? Stars above! THEY'VE GONE!

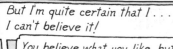

THE END